Under the Night Sun

Randy Lundy

Under the Night Sun

All Poems © Randy Lundy, 1999

All rights reserved. No part of this book covered by the copyrights herein may be reproduced or used in any form or by any means – graphic, electronic or mechanical – without the prior written permission of the publisher. Any request for photocopying, recording, taping, or storage in information storage and retrieval systems of any part of this book shall be directed in writing to: *CanCopy, One Yonge St., Suite 1900, Toronto, Ontario, M5E 1E5*

Edited by Patrick Lane.
Cover and book design by Duncan Campbell.
Typeset by Karen Steadman.
Cover illustration by Ray Keighley.
Printed and bound in Canada.

The publisher gratefully acknowledges the financial assistance of the Saskatchewan Arts Board, the Canada Council for the Arts, the Department of Canadian Heritage, and the City of Regina Arts Commission, for its publishing programme.

Canadian Cataloguing in Publication Data

Lundy, Randy, 1967–
Under the night sun
Poems.
ISBN 1-55050-155-0

1. Title.
PS8573.U5438U53 1999   C811'.54   C99-920141-7
PR9199.3.L863U53 1999

Coteau Books
401-2206 Dewdney Avenue
Regina, Saskatchewan
S4R 1H3

AVAILABLE IN THE U.S. FROM:

General Distribution Services
4500 Witmer Industrial Estates
Niagara Falls, New York,
USA, 14305-1386

for my mom and dad

*and that perfect goddess
whom I have tried, so imperfectly,
to love*

Contents

Bone-roots

1 ritual
2 as night holds
3 my touch
4 your touch
5 gifts
6 black crows
7 tonight i dream
8 a reed of red willow
9 sky-gift
10 westward memory
11 an answer to why
12 for my father
14 the only grace
15 you will wait

Impossible Flowers

19 i tried to hide
20 your beauty has been forgotten
21 impossible flowers
22 waking song
23 your body rises
24 body song
25 naked
26 sky-water song
27 last night s rain
29 you are a smooth stone
30 your body, a lake
31 as a stone remembers
33 last dream

Portraits

37 wolf
38 rob
40 billy the kid
42 anne
43 14 years old
44 20th street after dark
45 outside the albany
46 first times
47 the stinky blues
48 the story of an axe
49 the dangers of flight
50 i don't know where you are
52 just because

Moon-songs

61 Kise-pisim
62 Mikisiwi-pisim
63 Niski-pisim
64 Ayiki-pisim
65 Sakipakawi-pisim
66 Paskowihowi-pisim
67 Paskowi-pisim
68 Opahowi-pisim
69 Nocihitowi-pisim
70 Pinaskowi-pisim
71 Ihkowi-pisim
72 Pawacakinasisi-pisim

My Lodge

75 winter trees
76 dark forest
77 stone gathering
78 ghost dance
79 stone mother
80 hanging bones
81 for my mother
82 deer-sleep
84 the trees are spirits
86 elemental
88 my lodge

The word
was born in the blood
grew in the dark body, beating...

Pablo Neruda, "The Word"

Bone-roots

...as no tree listens I listened, and language
   came into my roots
            out of the earth
         into my bark
              out of the air,
         into the pores of my greenest shoots
              gently as dew...

Denise Levertov, "A Tree Telling of Orpheus"

ritual

this is a ritual, this uncovering of flesh
we shed clothes like tired skins
frost presses its face against the window

what are the words we should recite
the words this ceremony demands?

our tongues stir
deep roots reaching into earth
with no memory of sky

our hands move
new light on a landscape
coaxing a sound from silence

three thousand miles away
birds are beginning to flock

as night holds
    (for sheri b.)

april, the season hesitates
something slowly dies
some new thing quietly arrives

above, gulls, drifting ghosts
pale spectres drawn by moonlight
cries torn on the wind

an ecstasy keen as stars
sharp enough to draw blood
sever a finger, pierce a heart

your eyes, transparent green
last remnants of ice, melting
singing in the river

tonight, these are the only voices
untranslatable, my tongue stumbles
among stones on the bank

if i could speak a single word, perhaps
you would come

i would hold you as night holds
the river's curved, dark body

my touch

a dance of bird's feet
across wind-smoothed snow

your flesh shows no sign
no hieroglyph of descended flight

but the occasional stain of blood
betrays the path of mouth or hand

as if spring had awakened
in some lazy neighbourhood cat

a sudden new awareness
of teeth and claws

your touch

a flight of returning birds
their sudden, swift turn
a single motion
when they descend
a million feathered bodies
suddenly
everywhere

earth-flesh releases
a first breath

a warm rain sweeps across
the landscape my body is
wetness seeps
into hidden caverns
pools and sleeps
in curved bones

soft lips press
here and here
as leaves flutter down
scurry like mice
across my brown chest and belly
nestle under my chin
in the crook between my legs
where they gather to whisper

and then
a frost so hard
all that i am goes stiff
stilled
in an embrace that lasts
an entire season

gifts
> *(for sherry j.)*

i bring you
labrador tea and marsh marigolds
stories of tamarack
draped in moss and moonlight
mushrooms huddled between thick roots

you bring me
sage and sweetgrass
stories of sandhills
that stretch and recline, obliterate
the horizon, the separation of earth and sky

i dream
wind-shifted flesh
bleached the colour of bone
a sun close enough to touch

you dream
a slow river
a serpent that sheds its skin
a pearl and an opal for its eyes

black crows

this morning your eyes
two pools
thawed by sunrise

i see myself twice reflected
though i know you do not see me

your mind
a small, frightened bird, pursued
by the black crows of your dreams

they sit outside our window
in the twisted branches of an elm
staring in at your fluttering eyes
soft as the bodies of sparrows

i know they are still inside you
these hungry birds, black wings folding
each time you close your eyes

all day you are silent, distant
your head filled with voices, ancient voices
and the rustling of feathers, sharp beaks
preening sleek bodies

at the end of this day
we have lived alone

and it is time again
for the descent
the long, slow separation
of sleep

tonight i dream

the moon, hull of an ancient ship, founders
sinks into the trees, reefs of black coral

an ancient sailor
slips beneath the waves, drifts
in the deep seas of sleep

submerged in the thick scent
of sage and juniper, surrounded
by siren voices, songs of red and silver
willow and wind

he forgets love, and sex, and death

at dawn, the sun rises and spreads
a sail of light

a warm current washes
our naked bodies, together
upon the bed

and my desperate tongue searches
as if for a memory
for the salt upon your skin

a reed of red willow

a reed of red willow
stripped by the teeth of a beaver

white as stone in sun
slender as a flute

the notes it sings
into black night

white and slender
as a bone

in the wrist of a woman
you love

sky-gift
   (for shirley j.)

somewhere on the prairie
a dried lake bed, brown earth
caked and broken, by the breath
of white alkali and sun

the slope-backed hills
once fed this alluvial plain
but now, lost in dust-filled meditation
they have nothing left to offer

buried deep, beyond the reach
of memory, a prehistoric thirst
a single seed

carrying within
hidden light and potential colour
of a thousand prairie wildflowers

waiting only for the gift
the clarity of your touch

westward memory

barren fields
geese settle with the sun

the sight of so many wings
stops you
by the side of the highway

I stand behind, watch you
so beautiful, so close
my breath rises in clouds
freezes to your hair
obscures the horizon
so far away

back on the road
we travel westward
the earth buckles into mountains

still you are no smaller
only the sky is less

an answer to why

if you were to ask me
i would answer

it is the fault of the season

as the flesh of the trees is torn away
birds flee with the sun
removing their voices
far from our helpless ears

as the river moves toward stillness
bears dream themselves thin
among roots and stones

we too are part of this

for my father

the wind stretches tender wings
among last year's branches
and clinging leaves

the sound
a rattle of dried seeds

and you want simply
to say the names of things

sun and moon, tree and root

but you cannot remember
a single one
all things have taken back their names
and the rain whispers

nothing

the stones
which have overslept
begin to blink through snow
stoney-eyed, blind-white
stunned by revelations of light

a pale green in the trees
a few scattered wildflowers

as crocuses blossom and die
a patient sun climbs the sky

you try to awake
but again
you are enmeshed in the dream

your bones pale fish
adrift in an ocean of earth

and the underground water sings

sun and moon, tree and root

but you cannot remember the words

the only grace

you cannot answer
these small questions

where have the birds gone?
will they come back?

it is not a matter of maps and latitudes
and all afternoon the slow, dumb sky
has drained you

you are not even sure
the birds have followed the light
perhaps they have simply descended
into some greater night
a place where the sun never walks

even if you had a basket woven of willow
lined with sweet grass and human hair
in which to carry delicate bones
you havent been blessed with the gift
to follow them, to carry them back

so as evening settles
you sing this quiet song

it is the only grace
you have left

you will wait

you will wait
quietly, still and silent
as grass
just before dawn

slender green fingers
gathering dew from air

knowing when light comes
it will take back this gift
this offering night has made

knowing this
you will wait

for whatever there is to love
when light and darkness touch
on the horizon of your looking

Impossible Flowers

*your slightest look easily will unclose me
though i have closed myself as fingers,
you open always petal by petal myself as Spring opens
(touching skillfully, mysteriously) her first rose*

e.e. cummings, "Somewhere I Have Never Travelled,
Gladly Beyond"

i tried to hide
    (for your wild hair)

i tried to hide from love

i found myself lost
in the tangled vines of your hair, unkempt vineyard

fugitive, with teeth to puncture delicate skin
i have feasted heartily, tasted flesh and living seeds
fresh juices, distilled by sand and roots, fermented in sun

and now i am drunk, drunk and lost
fleeing through the shadows of your lashes
planted all neatly in rows

staggering, at last I find refuge
in your mouth, damp cavern, where my body lies heaving

but, even here, your breath
is the only air for my breathing

your beauty has been forgotten
   (for eva b.)

your beauty has been forgotten
an orchard long abandoned
by a generation gone to war

i am the one the war has forgotten
coward who hides in the forest
somewhere beyond the edge of your village

i will not bring you fruit, instead
i will bring you to this place
where no one comes to harvest

i will bring you to this sanctuary
where night severs fruit from boughs
with blades of silver starlight

i have been here many times
gathering fruit fallen in deep grass
heart and hands heavy as moonlight

i will place globes of fruit at your feet
dampened by constellations of dew
an offering of flesh for your lips

when the first bird sings the morning
you will remember each piece of fruit
i placed upon your tongue

impossible flowers

this morning, your eyes
impossible flowers in early spring

this morning, your brow
soft underside of a leaf

this morning, your lashes
tiny wings slowly beating

intimations of first flight

this morning i touch you
this gently

my breath upon your skin
falling like new light

waking song

the gentle light comes to my window
to gaze upon you sleeping quietly beside me

your breath moves soft and slow
sweet as the breath of white flowers

your eyes are small creatures of the sea
turning lazily in the warm waters of coral dreams

when your eyelids part and close and part again
two mouths speaking softly to the light

i struggle to understand
this secret language

i want to lend my voice
to this silent song of waking

your body rises

under the night sun of my mouth
your body rises to meet my touch

a slender shoot, a dream from the sleeping earth
a pale eye longing to see the sky

slow buds grow into sudden leaves
a blossom unfurls with a gasp

i would like to say i have spoken these colours
this green, this red, into the soft light that is everywhere

but i have never spoken
a word as gentle and fragile

as your body
rising to meet my touch

body song

buried deep inside
stones sunk in the dark earth

these words sing in your bones
a song rising from the marrow

naming the places of your body
your body of lands and skies and seas

your lashes the naked spines of trees
sway in the winds of your waking eyes

your brow and cheeks summon the sun
your breath an invisible flight of birds

here is the rolling heartland of your breast
the sweeping plain of your abdomen

the tangled undergrowth of your groin
between the curved ridges of your hips

the well-spring of sweet waters flowing
into the sinuous rivers of your thighs

these are the things i sing
my tongue a troubadour of the flesh

travelling with its little drum
down the archipelago of your toes

naked

naked, you are a bolt of lightning
slender stem of bluebells, peal after peal
of violet light

and the soothing showers that follow

naked, your lilac-flesh breathes
scent of roots and clay, and the deep green
of rain-heavy leaves

sky-water song

your touch is thunder and lightning
a slow summer rain, drumming
a sky-water song

the nails of your fingers, ten moons
travel my earth-brown flesh

every leaf of me trembles
in their light

days later
i carry your touch deep within

underground streams move and sing
bone-roots drink sweet waters
filtered through sand and clay

this clarity rises into my limbs
where feathers of preening birds
brush against my skin

last night's rain

with small hands the sky reaches down
to touch you in the night

small eyes watch from every angle
each minute movement of your body

small ears listen to your breathing
the green breath of budding leaves

sometime in the night, as we sleep
the rain comes quietly
to an end
the last few drops
cling to the sighing trees

but i still have not forgotten
your body

a river swollen beyond its banks
flooding through my dreams
carrying the moon
everywhere

in the morning
you wonder at my silence

i want to be
pure stillness, pure silence

a pool of rainwater
at the foot of a black elm
held in arms
of root and earth and sky

so when you look you will see
last night's rain
fallen as i have fallen
only to be close to you

you are a smooth stone

the river studies the moon
for ten thousand years

yearning to make something so perfect
so sad and mysterious

you are a smooth stone

lifted by the river's hands
placed upon the shore

a carved offering
between water and sky

your body, a lake

your body, a lake
my mouth, a night sky

constellations of teeth
a moon like a tongue

travelling the surface of water
staring into the depths

somewhere in the distance
tiny fish leap and disappear

a deer comes to drink
ears tuned to silence

the sound of water washing stones
polishing stones with hands of silver

the warm breath of your sighs
releasing memories of sun

feeding the night wind
wandering soft-footed among pines

as a stone remembers
 (for e.v.)

for a thousand years
water's supple body
descends
and
descends again
carving into the hard face of stone
a place of rest

at last
stone willingly cups
hands to hold
this sky-given grace

day after day
light gathers to drink

rain held in stone
shifts and changes form

the shape it leaves
a space in memory

this is how i remember you
as a stone remembers
water that has shaped its face

your image returns
to the place it has carved
always the same
always changing form
then is gone

and i wait
as a stone waits
until, almost forgotten
your soft body descends again

last dream

in that last dream before dawn

you come down from the mountain
walk slowly through the garden

your feet gather dew from the grass
where night wind has settled to rest

as i kneel to kiss them
each jewel trembles like flesh

your toes taste of morning and stone

Portraits

I have no damned words
    to make violence fit neatly
            like wrapped
            packages
of meat, to contain us safely.

    Joy Harjo, "Resurrection"

wolf

the first time you saw him
he was standing outside The Pat
in the 3:00 AM February cold
opening the door for drunk college kids
hoping for a bit of silver
for a moment something in you
reached out of the drunken haze
forgot the blonde you were trying to score
you dumped a handful of change
into the battered cap he held out
before stepping into a cab
with that girl you don't remember

today he's standing quietly
on the sidewalk outside the Commodore
as you step into the afternoon
after gorging yourself at the buffet
any other day you'd say hi
stop and ask about the family
the kids and the grandchildren
but today some woman in a business suit
is giving him hell
yesterday she saw him smoking
and yet here he is panhandling on the corner

she's a blonde
her face is strangely familiar

you pass by hoping he doesn't see you
when he calls out "Hey friend"
when he calls you by name
you look the other way

rob

you're in the alley having a smoke
he sidles up cautiously
half a pack of green weiners
protrude from his jeans pocket
like miniature missiles
loaded with nuclear waste
bags filled with cans and bottles
hang from each bony hand
cans and bottles bright and shiny
as the cars flashing by in the street

you offer a smoke
he relaxes a bit
talks about kids surfing the net
learning to build bombs
hole in the ozone

"gotta wear long sleeves
even in this heat"

talks about Conrad Black
global warming and the national debt

"it all has something to do with
people who throw out food
cans and bottles
instead of recycling
just like throwin' away money
what a crazy world"

he butts his smoke
and after pissing behind a dumpster
he thanks you and he's on his way
lotta ground to cover before dinner
well-boiled weiners and yesterday's paper

"lotta news to catch up on
what a crazy world"

billy the kid

as you sit on the bench
corner of 2nd and 21st
you hear the shuffle of his feet
different from the quick rhythm
of patent leather beneath business suits
he tells you his name

"billy the kid
that was my handle
back when I was a boxer"

outlaw, rebel, gunslinger

"my hands flew
like lead outta a six-shooter
my friends still call me that"

he decides to show you a few moves

"just in case anybody gives ya grief"

his bob and weave
a sway and a stagger
when he sees your doubt
he pops out his dentures

"where d'ya think my teeth went"

after that he was an impersonator

"my speciality was Orbison and Elvis"

popping his teeth back in
he dons a pair of dark glasses
sings a bit of "Jailhouse Rock"

winded from the effort
he asks for a smoke
you lie that you have none
he produces a concealed pack
offers you a Player's
and mumbles something about Hobbema

"oil money, too much money
drives people crazy"

offers to write you a cheque
just a thousand or two
then asks if you can help him out
just a quarter for some coffee

you reach into your pocket
past the bills to the silver
hand him sixty-two cents

anne

she sits down across from you
demands you buy her a beer
you tell her you're broke
"you're a fuckin' liar"
she tells you and she's right

since you want a beer
and she's not going anywhere
you go to the bathroom
come back with a story
20 bucks found on the floor
you order a couple of drafts
she introduces you to friends

when the 20 is gone
and you've both got a buzz on
you find yourself on the street
you help her search garbage cans
for plastic bags
you follow her down an alley
through an unlocked door
down a hallway lit by a single bulb
past a man asleep on a cot
she empties the freezer of meat
the bags are heavy and cold

back at the Barry
you peddle sausage and ground beef
but no one is buying today
the manager threatens to call the cops

back on the street
you follow her with your eyes
watch her shrink into the distance
balanced by a bag in either hand

14 years old

14 years old
high on glue or gas
she hangs with some friends
on a corner by the playground
beneath a streetlight that flickers

20 bucks for a blow
for 50 you can fuck her

her frail body conjures
cars from the suburbs
cars that dream the days away
in the darkness of parkades
beneath office towers

cars with tinted windows
insect eyes
in which she sees herself
until they slide down
without a sound

a hand groping in her pants

20th street after dark

in the alley behind the 7/11
pants halfway down to your knees
your dick in her mouth
and "oh it feels so good"

then her friend
who's been watching
and you liked it
says

"gimme yer munnie
or she bites it off"

all you can think is

how do i report this one?
armed robbery
weapon used?
teeth and tongue

fuck, what'll my wife say?
neither of them is older than 14
younger than my daughter
so young

all you can think is

how does this happen?
how do they get so tough?

"fuckin' little sluts"

outside the albany

four young men
cruising 20th
looking for hookers

a drunken woman
stumbles out of the Albany

the car slows to a crawl
they point and laugh

she gives them the finger
they laugh even harder

a quick trip around the block
just in time to see her fall

her face hits the pavement
                                      hard
and we laugh even harder

first times
   (for buryl b.)

sitting in the Barry
for the first time
your back against the wall
eyes alert
nervously scanning the crowd

you don't know
how it hurts me
to see you like this
nitotem

later we will laugh and joke
doing "The Indian Alphabet"
A-lbany, B-arry, C-onti
drinking Pil and Boh

but right now
looking at you
i see myself
ten years ago

sitting in the Northlands, in LaRonge
for the first time
my back against the wall
eyes alert
nervously scanning the crowd

the stinky blues
    (song overheard in The Conti)

mamma's in the whorehouse
and daddy's in jail

sister's on the corner, man
she's sellin' her tail

grandpa's in the backroom
he's gettin' laid

brother's sellin' coke
thinks he's got it made

come on, sing the stinky blues with me
come on, sing the stinky blues with me

(harmonica interlude and repeat
until someone buys you a beer)

the story of an axe
    (for johnny c.)

hiding under the bed
you hear the crash of the axe
unsure if it's a wall
or your mother's head
swallowing cold steel

you emerge
into the skinned-deer smell
of the room

did you turn on the lights
he so shyly extinguished
as he stumbled into the night?

when they find your father
he's still drunk
asleep beside a stump
which holds a bloody axe
in its woody fist

that morning
for the first time
you understood

the emptiness
he spoke of so often

the dangers of flight
 (for f.)

there once was a man
a magician of sorts
who taught women
the dangers of flight

when his wife
didn't come home for three nights
he dragged her by the hair
threw her through a window

the neighbors marvelled at this bird
that windows couldn't stop
her body arced through space
descended without grace

as curious eyes closed round
her bleeding body on the lawn
the second lesson had begun

her eldest daughter barely twelve

he closed his fist
around her bird-like wrist
dragged her screaming
to her mother's bed

the girl's cries
imitated her mother's flight
banged their beaks
on ceiling and walls

before collapsing
a heap of blood and feathers
on the floor

i don't know where you are

i have a way with words
a lyric gift
and a way of
backing it up with my fists

and i'm ready
to throw it all away
for a woman

and yet
i find myself
alone again
lost in the crowd
in the Albany

and i'm wondering
where you are
as i stagger on the dance floor

later, i sit
wearing a beret
dark glasses
and a fancy scarf
i'm bored
so i'm entertaining

the hooker insists
"he's gay"

the guy with the acid
defends me
convinced i'll buy
while his mother
with her baby jars
filled with Golden Wedding
is shocked

she can't believe
such a good looking young man
might be
"one of them"

and i'm ready
to throw it all away
for a woman

but i don't know
where you are

and i want to hit you

the way
my father hit my mother
the way
your father hit your mother
the way
he hit you
before you left him

i want to hit you
the way
i've never hit a woman
the way
i'm hitting
this stranger on the floor

i'm ready
with the gift of my fists
but i don't know
where you are

just because
    (for vanessa)

I

you got talking
just because
you were sitting alone
near the pool table
when they came in to play
and pretty soon
you were just talking

sometimes that's how it goes
there's no one else to talk to
so you talk to whoever's there
just because
you need someone to talk to

she's small
narrow shoulders and hips
no breasts or butt to speak of
almost delicate you would say
except for the blue ink
tattoos up and down her arms

he's just the opposite
thick and muscular
strong from many months behind bars
pumping iron to vent his anger
and just to stave off the boredom
the pool cue
a thin branch of willow
bends in his hands

she's smiling at you
and he doesn't like it

soon he has to go
he's on probation and has a curfew
"for stabbing some guy
who made a pass
when I wasn't looking"

she's going with him
but she's coming back in a while
"will you watch my beer for me?"

when she gets back two hours later
her face is bruised and swollen
"but I must of got some shots in"
she shows you her torn, bleeding knuckles
someone jumped her
but she didn't see who it was
at least that's her story

"oh well, shit happens"
and her beer is still full
sitting on the table
"so I know I can trust you"

and you know you shouldn't be
sitting so close to her
and don't kid yourself
it's not just pity
she's snuggling up
and her thin, hard body
feels so good

the bruises on her face
green, blue, and grey
against the background
of her deep brown skin
remind you of the banks of a river
colourful veins of clay
in the brown soil
her blood-red eye
a sun setting
just over the edge of the riverbank

II

when the bar closes
you head to her parents' place
the floor is littered with bottles
her father's passed out in his underwear
in the middle of the floor

no one else is around
so you follow her
carefully stepping over him

in the bedroom
you both load up with beer
and head back to the car

in an alley off twenty-second street
she climbs through the window of an apartment
you hand the beer in
and join her

you're not even finished your first
when friends begin to show up
someone has a bottle of vodka
and the last thing you remember
is chasing shots with beer

in the morning you wake
beside her on the couch
her vine-like body
curled around you

getting up for a beer
to chase away the hangover
you notice
all of the windows have been kicked in
neither of you remembers
how it might have happened

but that's just the way it goes sometimes
you wake up and find yourself
surrounded by violence
without any explanation

III

after the beer's gone
you head back to her parents'
and the party's in full swing

she introduces you
to her parents
to uncle so-and-so
to brothers and sisters
to nieces and nephews
and to her two young daughters
and you know this is wrong
that you shouldn't be here
that none of you should be here
but you stay anyway
just because

after sunset
you drive her to the Sally-Ann
to check on a friend
and you know it's the guy
from last night

before she gets out of the car
she hugs you
and her thin, hard body
feels so good
she kisses you
with her battered lips
and you can taste the salty blood
the way her skin tasted
last night
she makes you promise to wait

makes you promise
not to leave her here
"i can trust you right?"

once she's gone
you wait five minutes
and then drive away
and you can't say why

in the rear-view mirror
you see her step into the street
her lips are moving
she's saying something
but you can't hear her
and she knows it
but she's saying it anyway

it's the last time you see her

now you have this story
and you can't make any sense of it
so you just tell it
to whoever will listen

sometimes that's how it goes
there's no one else to talk to
so you talk to whoever's there
and hope someone will hear you
just because
you need someone
to hear the story

Moon-songs

> ...she knows
> what weight of body is, knows her flesh
> (her cells, her magic cell)
> mutters its own dark songs.
>
> Denise Levertov, "Fantasiestuck"

Kise-pisim
The Great Moon of Returning Hope (January)

the stars are tiny, scattered seeds
sending forth tendrils of light

you are the single, white blossom
vitrifying the land with your gaze

snow-laden branches
bend into shrines

where the winds circle
chanting softly

where small birds have left
three-toed offerings

Mikisiwi-pisim
   The Eagle Moon (February)

eagle-mother stares beyond
the long curve of the earth

deep into the reach of shadow
where purification is taking place

where sun lies drowsing
serpent in a bed of roots and stones

dreaming broad, strong wings
to lift sky from earth

Niski-pisim
The Goose Moon (March)

tonight sun comes mounted
upon the backs of snow geese

riding up from a land without light
to admire moon's blooming face

the river waxes full
preparing to shed a heavy skin

moon dreams her own image
reflected in a slow flow of water

Ayiki-pisim
   The Frog Moon (April)

these voices rise with the moon
waxing and waning in their throats

bright stone from the centre of the earth
rising through branches and bones

she is the song they sing
moon-song, song of slow light

pale asphodel
blooming in the night

Sakipakawi-pisim
The Budding Moon (May)

translucent husk of seed
thin bone of sacrifice

your fragrant light opens
the dark cavern of night

slender eyes on the branches of trees
wake slowly, soundlessly from sleep

your song brings a festival
green hands and feet

Paskowihowi-pisim
   The Hatching Moon (June)

moon shakes her cloak
and climbs
into a new body of light

you gather an offering of feathers
a bundle of blackened blossoms
plant them in the earth

later, in someone's dream
moon-stones grow
round and white as eggs

in the heat of a fire
they tremble and crack
releasing the voices of birds

Paskowi-pisim
The Moulting Moon (July)

moon digs a grave
deep in the shadow of the earth

her light
a thin sybilline voice
wanes
slowly into silence

whispers in hidden ears

you must fall
you must fall

birds shed feathers of grief
into the black hole of night

Ohpahowi-pisim
The Flying-up Moon (August)
(for debbie s.)

my heart flies up with the moon
small hand-drum in the night sky

skin scraped thin
tanned white
stretched tight
over bone

slow-beating song
at the centre of night

this is my gift to you
an offering of light

this sudden blossom
this unfolding of wings

Nocihitowi-pisim
The Mating Moon (September)

moon is in full bloom
yellow disc with six white petals

dressed in the plumage of love
she garners a last glance

as sun passes without a word
beyond the edge of the light

soon she will wander naked
giving birth again and again
to absence

Pinaskowi-pisim
The Migrating Moon (October)

it is a lie to say
the wind worships nothing
but emptiness

tonight
the wind is a lonely animal
raising a howl from the highest hill

searching the valley for moon's hidden face
buried in a bed of roots and leaves

overhead
the voices of eight ancestor-geese
trail the sun's southern journey

Ihkowi-pisim
    The Frost Moon (November)

moon's face has been veiled
three days and three nights

tonight
a slender splinter of hunger
remembering sun's far light

she is an owl made of snow
perched among frosted branches

dreaming
a thin blade of bone

a pool of blood
spilled on an altar of stone

Pawacakinasisi-pisim
The Frost-Exploding Moon (December)

i would like to say

nothing is forgotten
because nothing moves

then moon moves from behind
a heavy bank of snowclouds

the frozen landscape explodes
into light and silence

the green branches of a pine
the only voice in the night

My Lodge

*in the lodge
I lie and wait
heavy with birth,
plump with songs.*

Gregory Scofield, "Medicine Lodge"

winter trees
    (for e.a.l.)

winter trees
a stand of poplar and birch

turned inward, focussed on silence
at the centre of concentric rings

in another season
in preparation for the cold
roots, frantic fingers
gathered stones in the earth

in search of that single stone
prayer stone, medicine stone
a skeletal leaf locked inside
fossilized memory of light

for now, the winter trees wait

roots holding
an image of birth

bare branches
almost bone

dark forest

trees stretch
long shadows
across the sleeping forest floor

in this gathering of shadows
we mistake some for light
but there is not enough light

to call this shape owl
to call this shape fox

only the whispering

feathers stir the stilled air
furred feet bend dewed grass

our eyes are empty
our ears fill our heads

visions of teeth and talons

the stones are silent prophets
bone-white and waiting

stone gathering

stones gather in circles
on moonlit hilltops

with bowed heads they meditate
upon the things stones know

deep in forested valleys
there is singing and dancing

wind and shadows
honour these gathered stones

the stones inhale
ten thousand days

the stones exhale
ten thousand suns

into stone-sized
indentations in the earth

if we wait this long
will the guardians of beetle and worm

speak the secrets
of mountain and bone?

ghost dance

I

at sand creek, at wounded knee creek
the valleys are filled with bones

after the first green shoots of spring
when the wind stirs
the leaves and knee-high grasses
they will come, a gathering of many tongues

to hear of new soil coming like a tide
to greet the return of the buffalo
the herds of wild horses
the sound of thunder on the plains

they will dance and chant
from dawn until dawn
they will dance and chant
until they feel the earth move

II

the wind whistles a dry song
the sun touches the valley floor
the hills breathe a dusty breath

there is a shaking and rattling
tired bones coming together
each scattered part finding a place

brittle fingers gather
flesh of roots and moss
eyes of rounded stone

the laughter of the coming storm
shakes the world with its voice

stone mother

the parting, the opening
was not violent

i entered you
where you were sleeping

a crevice in your flesh
you did not know

eyes of light, eyes of air
entered there, and i pure
flowing water

your breath became cold
my touch became crystal, became ice

there in the slowest of silences
the soft centre of stone

you opened

hanging bones

i have hung hollow bones
with strands of braided hair
in the tangled branches of trees

the wind's voice
a song beneath the stars

bones of my people
hair of my head

moon brings her lantern
to witness shadows
spinning into dances

in early morning light
mosses and fallen leaves
stir quietly

the bones cry out

rise, rise with the dawn
be flesh
upon our cold, white bodies
we are not tired
we will carry you
we will carry you far

for my mother

a sky heavy with clouds
a bough burdened with snow

your tongue bends
to touch the frozen earth

the tracks of small animals have led you
into this sheltered place
you kill and roast their bodies
over a slow, green fire

when your hunger is fed
you suck marrow from thin bones
warm icicles in your mouth

now, perhaps, you can say
how memory lives in the bones
how it is possible

to swallow blood and marrow
to speak from this quiet centre

deer-sleep

this place does not require your presence
and beneath the staring stars
you have discovered
your offerings are meaningless

you are left with nothing
but silence

you have forgotten why you came here
you were looking for something

the wind wanders among willows
muttering forgotten stories
it has been everywhere and cannot
keep quiet

you must learn
to listen, to be alone

only then
will you bed down with the deer
to sleep in the long, deep grass
wrapped in the warmth
of slender bodies
of slow-moving breath

each time you awaken with the dawn
stars and moon fading memories
the deer will be gone

all day you carry with you
the sound of their sleeping

the howling song of coyotes
the common dream
that binds you

the trees are spirits

the trees are spirits
answering the call

wind and moonrise
conjuring from absence

these slow-swaying figures

and you too hear the call
come wandering

your belly-roots embracing
stone-heavy words

your throat
a slender flute carved from bone

clogged with river silt
and sleeping seeds

you came to this place
to unburden yourself

to raise your voice
into silence

you find only other voices
speaking words you have never heard

as you listen you forget
your half-remembered stories

how to begin and where to end

your heart a small drum beating
a bird's dreams of flight

the moon, your mind
gliding through trees   singing

elemental

your heart, a red moon
draws the tides of inner seas

your ancestors swim and sing
with the voices of whales

spawning fish gather
at the mouths of arterial rivers

follow memory

toward hidden lakes
pooled at the centre of bone

your blood is water
poured over
low-glowing, fire-heated stone
your blood is water
stones turn into air

something in you begins a journey

from thick salt seas
through thin skies of skin

your body moves
beyond itself

a black bird rises
broad wings stretch the night

and you are breathing
this slow-beating song

so that you may speak
some small thing

your body wants to speak

my lodge

this will be my lodge
skin stretched tight over bone

this I will call my home
sacred place I cannot leave

no light visits me
in this womb
thick with hot, stone-breath

moonlight beats
in the ear of the world

stars wonder
where I have gone

trees lean listening

my soft voice centred
........rises
........and
........falls
with the wind

Acknowledgements

Thank you, first of all, to my family and friends, who have always been there, especially to Buryl B., Laurie G., and Todd M., for providing continuity, and to Dottie, for her love and courage.

Thank you to the many others whose strength and determination showed the way; I will name only a few: Janice Acoose, Jeannette Armstrong, Maria Campbell, Beth Cuthand, Louise Halfe, and Greg Scofield. Thank you to everyone at Coteau Books for their impeccable taste and for making this possible. Thank you to Patrick Lane, for editorial advice and for his voice and vision, which have long been an inspiration. Thank you to Ray Keighley for the beautiful cover image. And, thank you to The Canada Council for the Arts, for the grant that made the writing of some of these poems a possibility and to the journals in which some of these poems first appeared.

About the Author

Randy Lundy has published poems and essays in a number of literary periodicals and scholarly journals. *Under the Night Sun* is his first book publication. He has an Honours English Degree from the University of Saskatchewan. He has worked as a sessional lecturer at the Saskatoon campus of the Saskatchewan Indian Federated College, and as writer-in-residence at the Regina campus of SIFC.

Randy is a member of the Barren Lands First Nation, based near Brochet, Manitoba. Born in Thompson, Manitoba, he lived in Quesnel, BC, and Hudson Bay, Saskatchewan before moving to Saskatoon in 1987.